The Carer Fairies

Three Stories in One

Join the Rainbow Magic Reading Challenge!

Read the story and collect your fairy points to climb the

Special thanks to
Rachel Elliot

ORCHARD BOOKS

Martha the Doctor Fairy first published in Great Britain in 2015 by Orchard Books
Ariana the Firefighter Fairy first published in Great Britain in 2015 by Orchard Books
Perrie the Paramedic Fairy first published in Great Britain in 2015 by Orchard Books

This collection first published in Great Britain in 2020 by The Watts Publishing Group

© 2015 Rainbow Magic Limited.
© 2015 HIT Entertainment Limited.
Illustrations © The Watts Publishing Group Limited 2015

ISBN 978 1 40836 407 9

MIX
Paper from
responsible sources
FSC® C104740
www.fsc.org

Orchard Books
An imprint of Hachette Children's Group
Part of The Watts Publishing Group Limited
Carmelite House, 50 Victoria Embankment, London EC4Y 0DZ

An Hachette UK Company
www.hachette.co.uk
www.hachettechildrens.co.uk
www.hachette.co.uk
www.hachettechildrens.co.uk

The Carer
Fairies

By Daisy Meadows

ORCHARD

www.rainbowmagicbooks.co.uk

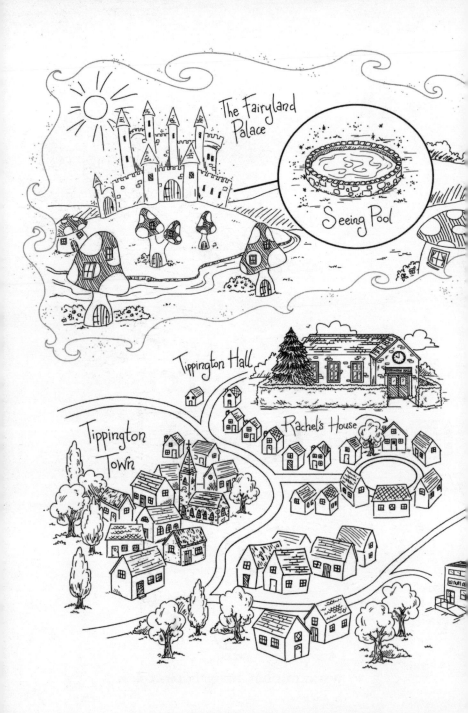

The Fairyland Palace

Seeing Pool

Tippington Hall

Rachel's House

Tippington Town

Jack Frost's
Ice Castle

Aunt Lesley's
Surgery

The Fire Station

Tippington Park

The Leisure Centre

Contents

Story One:
Martha the Doctor Fairy

Story Two:
Ariana the Firefighter Fairy

Story Three:
Perrie the Paramedic Fairy

Jack Frost's Spell

These silly helpful folk I see
Don't know they could be helping me.
But they will fail and I will smirk,
And let the goblins do the work.

I'll show this town I've got some nerve
And claim rewards that I deserve.
The prize on offer will be mine
And I will see the trophy shine!

Story One
Martha the Doctor Fairy

Chapter One
Medical Matters

"I love springtime," said Kirsty Tate, gazing out of the kitchen window with a dreamy expression on her face. "Everything looks as if it's been washed fresh and clean."

She finished drying the plate in her hands and passed it to her best friend,

Rachel Walker, to put away. Kirsty was spending half term in Tippington with Rachel and her family.

"Thanks for helping me, girls," said Rachel's dad, Mr Walker, who was washing up after the delicious breakfast he had made. "Many hands make light work."

"It's strange that Aunt Lesley didn't join us for breakfast," said Rachel, looking at the clock. "She's usually ready to leave for the surgery by now."

"How long is she going to be staying with you?" Kirsty asked.

"Just until the building work on her house is finished," said Rachel. "I hope it takes ages – I love having her here!"

"You're so lucky," said Kirsty. "She's amazing – I wish I had an aunt who was a doctor."

Rachel stacked a couple of glasses in the cupboard and then gave a little skip on the spot, feeling excited.

"It was brilliant hearing all about her work yesterday, wasn't it?" she said.

"Yes," Kirsty agreed, smiling, "and I loved learning how to take my own pulse with the second hand of my watch. I'm so glad that she's been nominated for the Tippington Helper of the Year Award."

The Helper of the Year Award was given to someone who had done something wonderful for the Tippington community.

"She's bound to win," said Rachel. "She's such an amazing doctor."

"Well, the other nominees are wonderful too," murmured Mr Walker with a smile. "We can't be sure that Aunt Lesley will win."

"I can," said Rachel in a determined voice. "She's unbeatable!"

Mr Walker laughed.

"You're right," he said. "I'm very proud

of her too. The most important thing of all is that her patients love her. That's the sign of a really good doctor, you know."

They finished the drying up and putting away, and then sat down at the table to practise taking their pulses again.

"Aunt Lesley's going to be late if she doesn't get up soon," said Rachel as she gazed at the kitchen clock.

"Why don't you two take her breakfast up on a tray?" said Mr Walker. "I bet she'd really be glad of that."

Kirsty went to get a tray, while Rachel filled a bowl with cereal and poured out some orange juice. They made some toast and added it to the tray with butter and honey, and then Rachel led the way upstairs and Kirsty carried the tray.

"Aunt Lesley?" called Rachel, knocking on the door of the spare room. "We've brought your breakfast up."

"Thank you, how kind!" said Aunt Lesley from inside. "Come in."

The girls opened the door. To their surprise, Aunt Lesley was still in bed. She was propped up with pillows, writing something and looking very relaxed.

"Are you working on the talk you're giving at the surgery later?" Kirsty asked, putting the tray down on Aunt Lesley's lap.

"Talk?" Aunt Lesley repeated in an

absent-minded way.

"Yes," said Rachel. "You told us about it yesterday – how you're going to explain all the things that doctors do in the community."

"Oh, hmmm," said Aunt Lesley. "No, this is a crossword puzzle. Do you know a six-letter word meaning a person who makes people well?"

"Doctor," the girls said in unison, exchanging a worried look.

"Aunt Lesley, are you OK?" asked Rachel. "Shouldn't you be getting ready for work?"

"I don't feel like going to the surgery today," her aunt replied.

"But your patients need you," said Kirsty, feeling shocked.

Aunt Lesley just shrugged as if she

didn't care.

"Do you feel poorly?" asked Rachel.

She put her hand on her aunt's forehead, but it wasn't hot. Kirsty took her pulse, but Aunt Lesley barely seemed to notice. Kirsty shook her head and pulled Rachel to one side.

"Your aunt's not poorly," she said in a low voice. "But she's not herself either. Whatever is the matter with her?"

Chapter Two
A Trip to the Seeing Pool

"Oh no!" exclaimed Aunt Lesley.

The girls looked around in surprise. Had she realised that her patients needed her?

"What's wrong?" Rachel asked.

"My pen's run out of ink," said Aunt Lesley with a groan. "This is terrible –

how can I finish my crossword? Oh girls, please would you run down and get another pen from my medical bag in the hall?"

The girls nodded and hurried back downstairs, feeling worried.

"I've never seen Aunt Lesley like this before," Rachel whispered. "Usually she can't wait to go to work."

Kirsty crouched down beside the bag and undid the catch.

"It's as if she's turned into a different person," she said. "Yesterday she couldn't stop talking about how much she loves being a doctor. Oh!"

Kirsty jumped up as a tiny fairy came fluttering out of the bag. Her red-gold hair was tied up with a blue ribbon, and she was wearing a white coat over her blue dress. A stethoscope was hanging around her neck.

"Good morning, Rachel and Kirsty," said the fairy. "I'm Martha the Doctor Fairy, and I need your help."

"Hello, Martha," Rachel whispered.

"We've just got to take a pen upstairs to my aunt. There's something not quite right with her this morning."

"I know all about your aunt," said Martha, nodding.

Before they could ask what she meant, the girls heard Aunt Lesley calling down from her room.

"Never mind about the pen," she said. "I'm going to go back to sleep. I feel like a nice long lie-in."

"Oh dear," said Rachel with a sigh.

"This isn't like Aunt Lesley at all."

"What did you mean when you said that you know all about Rachel's aunt?" Kirsty asked Martha.

"I can explain everything if you will come with me to Fairyland," said Martha.

The girls clasped each other's hands and nodded, smiling. No matter what the reason, it was always exciting to travel to Fairyland and visit their secret fairy friends.

While the girls pulled on their shoes and backpacks, Martha glanced around to check that no one was watching.

"It's OK," said Rachel. "Mum's gone out with a friend and Dad's making a cup of tea in the kitchen."

"Then let's go!" said Martha.

She flicked her wand and a dazzling swirl of sparkles surrounded the girls. They tingled with excitement as their wings appeared and they shrank to the size of fairies. Then fairy dust whooshed them into the air. One moment they were standing in the little hallway of Rachel's house, and the next they were blinking in the brilliant Fairyland sunshine.

"Welcome, girls, and thank you for coming," said a familiar voice.

It was Queen Titania, and she was smiling at Rachel and Kirsty. The girls curtsied at once.

"We're always glad when we can visit Fairyland," said Kirsty.

Looking around, they saw that they were standing beside the queen's Seeing Pool, in the grounds of the Fairyland Palace.

"Martha said that she needs our help," Rachel said.

"We all do," said a tinkling voice.

Rachel and Kirsty saw that three other fairies were standing beside the Seeing Pool.

"These are the other Helping Fairies," said Martha, stepping forward. "Girls, meet Ariana the Firefighter Fairy, Perrie the Paramedic Fairy and Lulu the Lifeguard Fairy."

The three fairies smiled at the girls.

"Queen Titania told us that you would come," said Ariana.

28

"Yes, you see, we don't know what to do," added Perrie. "Usually we help others, but now *we're* the ones who need help."

"What do you mean?" Kirsty asked.

"It's our job to take care of people who look after others in their community," Lulu explained. "But without our magical objects, we can't help the everyday heroes like Rachel's Aunt Lesley do their jobs. We can't help *anyone*. It's awful."

"Let me guess," said Rachel, frowning. "Jack Frost has stolen your magical objects? He's such a menace!"

The Helping Fairies nodded and Queen Titania raised her wand.

"Let's see if we can find out what he's doing now," she said.

Murmuring a powerful spell, she waved

her wand over the still water of the
Seeing Pool. It rippled and then a blurry
picture appeared.

"It's Jack Frost!" Rachel exclaimed as
the picture came into focus.

The Ice Lord was sitting at the top
of a snowdrift, and a crowd of goblins
was jostling for space below. Across his
chest was a satin sash in royal blue, with
the words 'HELPING
HERO' in large
white letters. As
the girls watched
he puffed out
his chest and
pointed to the
sash.

"Who do you
think is going to win

the Tippington Helper of the Year Award this year?" he bellowed at the goblins.

They scratched their heads, stared at each other and shrugged their shoulders.

"The Mayor?" suggested a knock-kneed goblin.

"A donkey?" said another.

"Me, you nincompoops!" Jack Frost shrieked. "ME! ME! ME!"

Chapter Three
A Sneaky Scheme

The goblins clapped and cheered.

"But how can *you* win an award for helping people?" piped up the smallest goblin, who was rather cheeky. "You're not really going to *help* people, are you?"

"Yuck, don't be disgusting," said Jack Frost. "I'll use the Helping Fairies' magical objects to make sure I win and everyone else FAILS! And besides, I've got all of you."

The goblins beamed with pride.

"We *are* very important, it's true," the smallest goblin squawked.

"Rubbish," said Jack Frost with an unpleasant smile. "But you're going to be doing the jobs of all the people nominated for the award, so that I can take the credit. That way *I* can win the award without actually having to help anyone!"

The watching fairies gasped, but the silly goblins didn't seem to understand that this meant more work for them. They clapped and cheered, and Jack Frost sat and laughed at them.

"What do you want us to do first?"

asked one of the goblins.

"Each group of goblins must come and collect one of the magical objects," Jack Frost ordered. "Then push off to the human world and win that award for me!"

The silly goblins clapped and cheered again, and then started to scramble up the slippery snowdrift. Jack Frost handed the smallest goblin a chunky white watch.

"My magical watch!" cried Martha.

The second group, led by the knock-kneed goblin, took Ariana's magical helmet. The third group, led by another goblin, took Perrie's magical flashing siren. The remaining goblins, who were all rather pimply, took off with Lulu's magical whistle.

"They've got our magical objects," said

Perrie with a groan.

"So *that's* what's wrong with Aunt Lesley," Rachel realised. "She's stopped wanting to look after people because the magical objects have been stolen."

Martha nodded. "My magical watch

makes sure that doctors give people good advice," she said. "Without it, doctors won't even *want* to help their patients."

"Now disappear to the human world

and get to work!" Jack Frost squawked, waving his wand.

The goblins vanished with a blast of icy magic. Then the picture in the Seeing Pool started to shiver and break up, and Queen Titania lowered her wand.

"That's all I can see," she said in a sad voice. "I cannot tell where the goblins have been sent. All we can know for sure is that they are somewhere in Tippington."

"Then we need to get home straight away," Rachel said.

"So you'll help us?" asked Lulu.

"Of course," said Kirsty. "We'll do everything we can to get your magical objects back before the prize is awarded."

"In that case, there's no time to lose," said Martha. "Back to Tippington!"

She flourished her wand and the girls were once more surrounded by swirls of fairy dust. A few moments later, feeling a little dizzy, Rachel and Kirsty were standing in a narrow alleyway.

"We're human-sized again," said Kirsty.

"Yes, and we're back in Tippington," Rachel replied.

"This is the alleyway next to Aunt Lesley's surgery. Why have you brought us here, Martha?"

Martha was fluttering beside them, biting her lip and looking anxious.

"I think this is where the goblin with my magical watch will come," she said. "Jack Frost sent the goblins to do the jobs of all the people nominated for the award."

"We have to try to keep the goblins away from Aunt Lesley's surgery," said Rachel. "They could cause all sorts of mischief!"

Martha hid inside Kirsty's backpack, and then the girls walked out of the alleyway and up the steps to the surgery. As soon as they pushed the door open, they were stopped in their tracks by the noise. The waiting room was filled with patients who were grumbling, shouting, coughing and sneezing. Each one was holding a number, and the receptionist was trying to keep them all calm, enter their details into the computer and answer the phone – all at the same time.

"Hi, Uma," said Rachel, walking up to the reception desk.

"Oh Rachel, I'm so glad to see you," said Uma. "Is your aunt feeling better? Her talk is due to start soon, and the replacement doctor is giving patients some ... er ... very strange advice!"

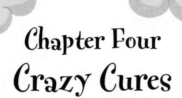

Chapter Four
Crazy Cures

Just then, a man came out of the examining room, hopping on one foot. Uma stood up and looked at him in surprise.

"Excuse me, sir," she called after him. "I don't remember you hopping when you went into the room – I thought you came in for a cold. Are you all right?"

"I soon will be," said the man. " The doctor says it'll cure my cold in an hour."

"See what I mean?" said Uma as the man left the surgery and the next patient went into the examining room. "I've never heard a doctor say that before."

Kirsty and Rachel exchanged glances. Was it possible that the goblins were already here? Uma asked the caller to ring back and put the phone down.

"Er, Uma, what's the new doctor like?" Rachel asked.

The phone rang again. Uma picked it up and put her hand over the receiver.

"He seems quite young for a doctor," she said. "And he has extremely large feet. Oh, excuse me, I really must answer this call."

"Kirsty, are you thinking what I'm thinking?" asked Rachel.

Kirsty nodded. "It sounds like a goblin in disguise," she said. "But we have to get into the examining room and meet him to be sure."

Rachel looked around at all the angry patients.

"It'll take hours to get in if we join the queue," she said. "We have to do something quickly. Martha, I think it's time for us to become fairies again!"

Rachel and Kirsty slipped behind a large pot plant, and then Martha fluttered out of Kirsty's backpack and flew above the girls, waving her wand.

Dazzling fairy dust showered down on the girls, and they instantly shrank to fairy size. A few seconds later they were fluttering beside Martha and peering out from behind the pot plant.

"Look – the examining room door is opening," Kirsty whispered.

A lady walked out, singing *Hickory Dickory Dock* backwards. In the waiting room, a lady stood up and beckoned to her son.

"Come on, Josh!" she said. "It's our turn at last."

As Josh and his mum walked into the examining room, the three fairies flew in above them. The door shut, and the fairies perched on a tall cupboard.

For a moment, Rachel and Kirsty didn't even look at the doctor. They were too busy staring at the terrible mess. Papers and files were scattered all around the room. Medical equipment covered the floor and the desk, and Aunt Lesley's computer was flashing with a big warning signal.

"This is terrible," said Rachel. "Aunt Lesley always keeps her examining room neat and tidy. She'd be really upset to see this."

The girls couldn't see the doctor's face

because he was wearing a wide-brimmed hat, but Kirsty pointed to his enormous feet and nudged Rachel and Kirsty.

"His feet are much too big," she said. "I think he's a goblin in disguise."

Then they heard a
squawk from the
far corner of
the room,
and saw a
group of
other goblins
in hats and
white coats,
messing
around with
thermometers
and stethoscopes. Martha let out a
little groan.

"Ahem," said the doctor goblin, putting
on a silly, deep voice. "Sit down and, er,
start moaning ... no ... I mean, tell me
what's wrong."

"Isn't it obvious?" asked Josh's mum.

She and Josh sat down, and the fairies saw that he was covered in spots. The doctor goblin rubbed his hands together.

"Is it because he's so ugly?" he asked. "I can't do anything about the nose, but we could pluck his eyebrows …"

"His spots!" exclaimed Josh's mum.

"Oh yes, of course," said the doctor goblin with a nervous giggle. "Well, it's probably a cold, but I need to take his pulse."

He pulled a chunky
white watch out of his
pocket and Martha
gasped.

"My watch!" she
said, leaning forward
over the cupboard.
"It's here!"

"And we have to
get it back," Kirsty
added. "But how?"

The goblin doctor held the watch
upside down and pressed it against Josh's
forehead, before putting it carefully back
into the pocket of his coat. Josh's mum
frowned.

"I thought it was probably chickenpox,"
she said.

"That's right," said the goblin doctor.

"Chickenpox, definitely."

He nodded so much that his hat fell off. He snatched it up and plonked it back on his head. Josh's mother stared at him.

"Yes," he squawked. "Chickenpox."

"So what should I do to help him?" Josh's mother asked.

"He should stand on his head three times a day after meals," said the goblin doctor. "NEXT!"

Josh immediately leaned over as if to try straight away. But his mother pulled him to his feet.

"I've never heard such utter nonsense," she said. "I'm not coming back here again until Dr Lesley returns."

She stomped out and the goblin doctor blew a loud raspberry at her back. Kirsty tapped Martha on the arm.

"I've got an idea," she whispered. "But you'll have to turn us both back into humans again."

Chapter Five
Rainbow Pox

A few seconds later, Rachel and Kirsty stepped out from behind the cupboard and walked up to the doctor as if they were his next patients. Rachel pretended to sneeze … and sneeze … and sneeze.

"Help!" Kirsty exclaimed. "I think my friend has sneezitis. She's sneezing nonstop – can you help her? Can you take her pulse?"

"No need for that," said the goblin doctor, waving his arm. "The best cure for sneezitis is to clap your hands and stamp your feet."

Kirsty bit her lip. The goblin doctor stared at Rachel, who kept sneezing. There was nothing else for it – she started to clap her hands and stamp her feet.

As the goblin doctor stared at Rachel, Kirsty had another idea. She whispered to Martha, who was hiding in her backpack, and the little fairy waved her wand. A ribbon of fairy dust twirled its way across the room and up the nostrils of the goblin doctor.

"AH-CHOO!" he burst out.
"AH-CHOO! AH-CHOO!"

Rachel stopped sneezing and stared
at the goblin doctor, whose eyes were
beginning to water.

"AH-CHOO! AH-CHOOO!"

"Oh my goodness, you must have
caught the sneezitis!" Kirsty exclaimed.
"Now *you're* going to
have to clap your
hands and stamp your
feet!"

As the doctor
goblin started to
clap and stamp,
Martha slipped
out of Kirsty's
backpack.

With all the sneezing, clapping and
stamping, the doctor goblin couldn't see
anything, and the other goblins were busy
drawing pictures on prescription forms.
It should have been easy for her to dive
into the doctor's coat to get the magical
watch. But when Martha got close to the
pocket …

"AH-CHOO!"
A gigantic sneeze
shook the goblin
doctor's body,
and he moved
out of Martha's
way. She
fluttered closer to
the pocket again,
but just as she was
about to fly inside …

"AH-CHOO!" He turned to hold on to his desk. The plan wasn't working.

"We have to think of something!" cried Kirsty.

Suddenly Rachel remembered the doctor goblin's strange cure for Josh's chickenpox.

"I've got an idea!" she exclaimed. "Martha, hide under my hair and I'll whisper to you."

Martha darted out of sight, and smiled as she listened to Rachel's plan. Then she waved her wand and the goblin doctor stopped sneezing. Martha took a deep breath and chanted a quick spell.

Goblin, goblin, grow some spots.
Big ones, small ones, lots and lots.
Goblin, though your skin is green,
In rainbow colours now be seen.

With that, a rash of
rainbow-coloured spots
appeared all over the
doctor goblin's face.
Rachel gasped and
Kirsty put her hand
to her mouth.
"Oh my goodness,
you must have rainbow
pox!" she exclaimed. "It's the worst case
I've ever seen!"

Rachel pulled the goblin doctor over to
a mirror on the wall, and he gawped at
his face in horror.

"Look at me!" he shrieked at the other goblins. "Help!"

But the other goblins just pointed at him and rolled around the floor laughing. Kirsty gave him a comforting pat on the back.

"There, there," she said. "The cure for rainbow pox is the same as for chickenpox – you have to stand on your head."

Panting and gibbering to himself about spots, the goblin doctor did a headstand. Just as Rachel had planned, Martha's magical watch came tumbling out of his pocket!

Chapter Six
Helping Hands

"Look out!" squawked the other goblins, diving towards the magical watch.

"Too late," said Rachel, pouncing on the watch. "It's time that this was returned to its rightful owner."

As the goblins jumped up and down in fury, Martha flew out of hiding and took

the watch, which
magically shrank
to fairy size.

The goblins
groaned, but the
goblin doctor
was on his feet
again and gazing
into the mirror.

"It hasn't worked!" he
wailed. "I'm still all poxy!"

"Spots are going to be the least of
your worries when Jack Frost finds out
what's happened!" one of the other
goblins yelled. "The fairy's got her
watch back, you idiot! Come on, we've
got to hide."

The other goblins opened the window
and clambered out, but the doctor

goblin stared at Martha. His bottom lip trembled.

"I want my handsome green face back," he whimpered.

With a wave of Martha's wand, the rainbow spots vanished. The goblin doctor heaved a sigh of relief, and then pulled off his white coat and hat.

"I suppose I am not a very good doctor after all," he said to the fairies in a croaky voice.

"Never mind," said Martha with a
bright smile. "I have just the thing to
make you feel better."

She tapped her wand on his chest, and
a sticker appeared there.

I was very brave at the doctor's today.

The goblin grinned
and then followed
the others out
of the window.
Martha turned
to the girls with
a little laugh.

"What
an exciting
morning!" she said.
"Thank you from
the bottom of my heart. I have a little
something for you too."

She tapped their chests with her wand, and two more stickers appeared with rainbow-coloured writing.

Doctor's Helper

"Thank you," said Rachel, gazing at her sticker. "It was a pleasure to help!"

"I must take my magical watch back to Fairyland," said Martha. "But please keep an eye out for the other three magical objects."

"We will," Kirsty promised her. "Goodbye!"

There was a bright, silvery flash that made the girls shut their eyes. When they opened them again, Martha had disappeared and the examining room was as neat as it had always been. No one could have guessed that goblins had been there a few minutes earlier.

"Perfect," said Rachel. "Come on, let's go home and wake Aunt Lesley up."

They went back into the waiting room, but they were surprised to see that all the patients had disappeared. Instead, the waiting room chairs were laid out in rows, and people were filing in to take their seats for the talk. Uma smiled at the girls and beckoned them over to the reception desk.

"I've just been speaking to your aunt," she said. "Wonderful news! She's feeling much better and she's on her way to work!"

An hour later, Kirsty and Rachel were sitting in the front row as Aunt Lesley came to the end of her talk. Every seat was filled, and some people were even crowding around the edges of the waiting room so they could listen.

"Finally, I would like to say that one of the most important things you need to be a good doctor is to love what you do," said Aunt Lesley. "Nothing gives me more happiness than helping my patients to feel better."

Everyone burst into applause and Aunt Lesley made her way over to the girls.

"Will you help me?" she asked them. "I want to show the children in the audience how to take a pulse and use a stethoscope."

"Of course," said Rachel and Kirsty at once, feeling proud to be asked.

As they started to demonstrate to the other children, they saw Josh's mother tap Aunt Lesley on the shoulder.

"That was a wonderful talk," she said. "I was wondering – what do you think about standing on your head as a cure for chickenpox?"

The girls flashed a smile at each other, and Aunt Lesley laughed.

"I can't say I've ever heard of it," she said. "Chickenpox usually gets better on its own, but I can give you some special lotion for the itching."

"Thank you, that would really help," said Josh's mother. "Good luck for the Tippington Helper of the Year Award."

As Josh's mother walked away, Rachel had an idea. She looked up at her aunt.

"Aunt Lesley, we'd really like to meet the other nominees for the award," she said. "Do you think that might be possible?"

"Of course," said Aunt Lesley at once. "They're all lovely people. I'll take you this week."

She turned aside to speak to Uma, and Kirsty squeezed Rachel's hand.

"Good thinking," she said. "It's brilliant that Martha has got her magical object back, but we've still got three more objects to find."

Rachel nodded. "We have to make sure that helpers in the community are there for the people who need them," she said. "Hopefully we'll be able to find the other magical objects very soon!"

Story Two
Ariana the
Firefighter Fairy

Chapter One
Calamity Kitten

The kitchen was filled with the clatter of cups and plates and the smell of toast – the Walker family had just finished breakfast.

"It's another gorgeous spring day," said Rachel Walker, stepping out of her back door into the garden. "I'm so glad we don't have to sit inside a classroom today."

Her best friend, Kirsty Tate, followed her and took a deep breath of fresh air. She was staying with Rachel in Tippington for half term. The kitchen window opened and Mrs Walker leaned out to call to them.

"Girls, please would you water the

plants while you're out there?" she asked. "They need extra care in all this heat."

It had been a wonderfully sunny half term so far.

Rachel and Kirsty filled their watering cans and started to water the beautiful plants. The spring bulbs were flowering and scenting the air.

Just as Kirsty was watering the tulips, she heard a faint sound. Rachel heard it too, and stopped beside the daffodils to listen.

"It's a meow," said Kirsty. "There must be a cat in the garden. Come on, let's find it!"

They put down their watering cans
and searched among the bushy plants
and behind the plant pots, but there was
no sign of a cat. Then Bailey, the little
boy who lived next door, popped his
head over the fence. He looked worried.

"Rachel, please will you help me?" he
called. "My kitten, Pushkin, has climbed
on top of the shed in your garden, and
now she's stuck!"

"Of course we will," said Rachel at
once. "Don't worry, Bailey – we'll get her
down."

They walked to the little green shed
at the end of the garden, where the
lawnmower and gardening tools were
kept. On the roof, they could see a
pair of large, scared eyes peeping down
at them.

"Come on, puss," said Rachel in a gentle voice. "Don't be scared – you can get down."

Pushkin took a step back.

"Maybe she'll come down to eat something," said Kirsty thoughtfully. "Bailey, could you go and get some of her favourite food?"

Bailey nodded and disappeared from view. The tiny tabby kitten was letting out little meows and crouching flat against the roof.

She took a step closer to the edge of the roof and meowed again. Bailey's head popped back up, and he held out a dish of cat food over the fence.

"Come on, Pushkin," Rachel called. "Look, it's your favourite. Time to come down."

She held out her hand, and Pushkin gazed at her for a long time. Then, just when it seemed as if she might stay on the roof for ever, the little kitten plucked

up her courage and jumped down onto
the fence. For a moment she looked a
little wobbly.

"You can do it, Pushkin," called Kirsty.

Pushkin leaped down into Bailey's
garden. He let out a delighted cheer.

"Thank you, Rachel!" he called.
"Thank you, Kirsty!"

"No problem," said Rachel, smiling at

the little boy. "We're just glad she's safe."

"She loves climbing things," said Bailey with a grin. "She's always getting stuck, though."

The girls hung over the fence and watched as Pushkin ate her food. Then Bailey picked up the kitten and the dish, waved to the girls and headed back inside his house. Rachel and Kirsty smiled at each other.

"Aunt Lesley's right," said Rachel. "It's a great feeling to be able to help people."

"Helping Bailey and Pushkin was almost as good as helping the fairies," said Kirsty in a low, happy voice.

Rachel and Kirsty had often visited Fairyland, and they loved being able to help their magical friends when Jack Frost caused trouble for them. Right

now they were caught up in one of
their biggest fairy adventures ever. Jack
Frost had stolen the magical objects that
belonged to the Helping Fairies, and the
girls had promised to try to find them.

Rachel's Aunt Lesley was a doctor,
and she had been nominated for the
Tippington Helper of the Year Award.
Yesterday, she had been acting very
strangely until the girls had returned
Martha the Doctor Fairy's magical
watch to its rightful place. There were
still three objects to find, and time was
running out.

Chapter Two
A Garden Visitor

The award ceremony was later that week, and the girls knew that if they hadn't found the magical objects by then, it would be a disaster.

The Tippington Helper of the Year Award was a local prize that was given to a special person in the community whose job it was to help others. Rachel's Aunt Lesley was staying with the Walkers while some building work was being done on her house, so Rachel and Kirsty had heard all about her work and how much she enjoyed helping people.

"I almost wish we could tell Aunt Lesley about the Helping Fairies and Jack Frost," said Rachel as she went to the outside tap to fill up her watering can again.

"Stop!" cried Kirsty, as Rachel was reaching her hand out to the

tap. "Your watering can is glowing!"

Hastily, Rachel put the watering can down and watched as the glow inside it grew brighter and brighter.

"Do you think it's a fairy?" she asked in excitement.

Kirsty nodded, too thrilled to speak. Seconds later, Ariana the Firefighter Fairy came fluttering out and perched on the spout. The girls remembered her from their meeting in Fairyland the day before.

91

"Good morning, girls!" she said in a
bright voice. "I'm hoping
that I can find
my magical
firefighter's
helmet today.
Will you help
me?"

"Of course
we will!" said
Kirsty at once.

She and Rachel
knew that without
their magical objects, the Helping Fairies
couldn't help everyday heroes like Aunt
Lesley do their jobs. Jack Frost wanted
to win the Tippington Helper of the Year
Award himself, but he wasn't prepared
to do any helping! Instead, he had sent

his mischievous goblins to do the jobs of
all the award nominees. He planned to
pretend that he had done the jobs himself
so that he could win.

"I just don't know where
to start looking," said
Ariana, holding out
her arms. "How are
we ever going to
find the goblins?"

"Don't give up,"
said Kirsty, smiling
at the little fairy.
"We got Martha's
watch back and now
Rachel's Aunt Lesley is
helping her patients again.
We'll find your helmet too."

"Yesterday, the goblins took Martha's

magical watch to Aunt Lesley's surgery,"
said Rachel in a thoughtful voice. "I
wonder if they could have taken your
helmet to the fire station."

Kirsty looked anxious.

"The goblins could cause serious
trouble at the fire station," she said. "We
have to get the helmet back quickly, or
the firefighters won't be able to do their
jobs."

"I've got an idea," said
Rachel. "Dad told me
that there's an open
day at the fire
station today. Let's
ask if we can go
and look around.
If the goblins are
there, I'm sure we'll

see them. They're not very good at
keeping out of sight!"

"That's a wonderful idea!" cried Ariana.
"Let's go!"

Ariana whooshed through the air and
dived into Kirsty's
pocket to hide.
Then the
girls ran
towards
the house
to find
Mrs Walker.
But when they
burst through the
back door into the kitchen, Mrs Walker
was nowhere to be seen. Aunt Lesley
was there, working on her computer at
the kitchen table. She looked up when

Rachel called to her mum.

"Your mum's popped out to the shops," she said. "She asked me to keep an eye on you while I'm updating my patient files."

"Oh no," groaned Rachel. "We were

hoping to go to the open day at the fire station. Dad said that they're holding demonstrations of firefighting."

Aunt Lesley closed her laptop.

"That sounds interesting," she said.
"I've actually just finished my work – it
didn't take as long as I expected. I'd be
delighted to take you to the fire station, if
you'd like to go with me instead?"

"That would be amazing!" said Kirsty.
"Are you sure?"

"Of course!" said Aunt Lesley. "It'll be a

chance to see my old friend Isobel, who
works there. She's been nominated for
the Tippington Helper of the Year Award
too."

Kirsty and Rachel exchanged a
knowing look. If
Isobel was one of
the nominees,
then the goblins
would probably
be trying to
take over her job.
It was lucky that
Aunt Lesley knew her
and could introduce them.

"We'll go in my car," said Aunt Lesley.
"I'll just write a note to tell your mum
where we've gone."

A few minutes later, Kirsty and Rachel

were sitting in the back of Aunt Lesley's car and they were zooming towards the fire station.

Chapter Three
Fearful Firefighters

"Is Isobel a firefighter, Aunt Lesley?"
Rachel asked.

"Yes," said Aunt Lesley. "Other people
run away from fires, but she puts on
her helmet and her equipment and runs
into them."

"She must have a lot of courage," said

Kirsty in awe.

"Isobel is the bravest person I know," said Aunt Lesley. "She has saved so many lives and helped so many people, I've lost count."

They arrived at the fire station and Aunt Lesley parked the car. There was a large crowd of people in the courtyard in front of the building.

"Look, there are lots of people here for the open day," said Rachel, clambering out of the car.

There was a pretend building in the middle of the courtyard.

"I expect they'll use that for the demonstrations later," said Aunt Lesley.

"But where are all the firefighters?" asked Kirsty, looking around.

There wasn't a single firefighter to be seen, even though it was past the start time for the open day.

"Let's go inside the fire station," said Aunt Lesley. "I want to show you something."

When they walked inside the building, the first thing they saw was a shiny silver pole that reached up through the ceiling.

"The firefighters slide down this pole when there's an emergency call," said Aunt Lesley. "It's here so they don't waste time running down the stairs, and they can get to the fire as quickly as possible."

"It looks like fun," Kirsty whispered to Rachel.

Rachel grinned back at her.

"I wish we could have a go," she said.

They all looked up to the top of the fire pole and saw several worried faces staring down at them.

"Isobel!" exclaimed Aunt Lesley, sounding very surprised. "What are you doing up there? There are lots of people here for your open day. Come on down."

Rachel and Kirsty looked more closely and saw that the people at the top of the pole were in uniform. They were all firefighters.

"We can't," said

Isobel in a trembling voice. "It's too far."

"What do you mean?" asked Aunt Lesley, confused. "Just slide down the pole."

"Ooh, no, I couldn't," said Isobel. "I don't like heights."

"It makes me dizzy just thinking about it," squeaked a big, burly firefighter.

"I can't look," said another, squeezing his eyes shut.

"I can't understand it," said Aunt Lesley to the girls. "Is it some sort of joke?"

"I don't think they're joking," said Kirsty, exchanging a secret glance with Rachel.

They both knew exactly why the firefighters weren't feeling very brave. They wouldn't have the courage they needed to do their jobs until Ariana's

magical helmet was back in Fairyland
where it belonged.

Suddenly there was a deafening noise
from the fire engine outside the fire
station. Its siren blared and all its lights
started flashing. Aunt Lesley barely
seemed to notice the noise – she was too
worried about her friend.

"I'm going up to
see if I can help
Isobel," she said.

She started up
the stairs, and
Kirsty and
Rachel ran
outside to
see what was
happening. Four
firefighters were

climbing out of the fire engine, swinging themselves down like acrobats while the crowd cheered and clapped.

"I've never seen firefighters in a green uniform before," said Rachel. "Even their boots are green."

"They must be goblins!" gasped Kirsty.

Chapter Four
A Drenching Demonstration

When she heard what Kirsty said, Ariana peeped out of the pocket where she was hiding.

"You're right," she whispered to the girls. "Look at that plump goblin on the end. He's wearing my magical helmet!"

Each goblin was wearing a helmet with

a large visor that covered his face. Three of the helmets were green, but the fourth was yellow and sparkling in the spring sunshine.

"We *have* to get that helmet back," said Rachel, squeezing her hands into fists. "Until it's returned to Fairyland, the real firefighters won't have any courage, and they won't be able to protect people."

"But how can we get the helmet back?" asked Ariana. "It just seems impossible."

"Nothing is impossible," Rachel replied. "We'll find a way!"

Just then, the plump goblin wearing Ariana's magical helmet grabbed a hose.

"Time for a demonstration!" he squawked.

112

He climbed up the ladder of the
practice building with a hose and
showered the other
goblins with water.

"Hey, stop it!"
screeched the
other goblins.
"You'll be
sorry!"

They
grabbed
hoses too,
and within
seconds they
had started a
massive water
fight. Water sprayed over the
crowd and soaked everyone, including
Rachel and Kirsty.

People laughed at first, but after a few minutes they started to get annoyed.

"This isn't much of a demonstration!" said one man.

"There wasn't even a fire to put out," a lady grumbled.

"Stop!" shouted a young mother.

But the goblins took no notice until the loudspeaker in the courtyard let out a loud squeal.

"Emergency! Emergency! A kitten is stuck up a tree. Firefighters required! Hurry!"

The goblins flung down their hoses and raced to the fire engine.

"To the rescue!" bellowed the plump goblin.

With the siren wailing, the fire engine zigzagged towards the crowd, trailing its

hoses behind it. People scattered
as it lurched out of the courtyard,
turned sharply and hurtled off down the
road, with goblins hanging on to it for
dear life.

"How are we going to get the helmet
back now?" Kirsty asked.

"We need to follow the fire engine," said Rachel. "Ariana, can you turn us into fairies? The only way to catch up with those goblins is to fly after them!"

"Of course!" said Ariana. "But you'll need to hide somewhere so that I can transform you."

The girls looked around and Kirsty grabbed Rachel by the hand.

"The garage," she said. "It's empty now. Come on!"

They ran into the deserted fire engine garage, and Ariana flew out of Kirsty's pocket. She flourished her wand and a puff of fairy dust sprinkled down on the girls. They instantly shrank to fairy size.

"I love flying!" said Rachel, spinning into the air and scattering fairy dust from her fluttering wings.

Kirsty twirled up beside her, and Ariana joined them. For a moment, everything was forgotten except the joy of flying on glimmering fairy wings. Then Rachel clapped her hands together.

"Let's catch that fire engine!" she exclaimed.

Flying high so that they wouldn't be spotted, the fairies zoomed in the direction the fire engine had gone.

117

Luckily the goblins didn't know much about driving a fire engine, and it was slowly zigzagging along, only just staying on the right side of the road.

"It's heading towards your house, Rachel!" Kirsty cried.

With a squeal of brakes, the fire engine stopped just before Rachel's home. Bailey came running out of his house, looking tearful.

"Thank you for coming!" he called to the goblin firefighters. "My kitten can't get down!"

The goblins climbed out of the fire engine on wobbly legs.

"Where's the problem?" said the plump goblin in the magical helmet.

Bailey pointed at the tall oak tree that grew opposite his house.

"She's on a branch up there," he said. "Please help her."

The goblin puffed out his chest and started snapping out orders at the other goblins.

"Get a ladder! Put it up against the tree! Not like that, you idiot!"

"Who does he think he is, Jack Frost?" grumbled one of the other goblins as the fairies fluttered over their heads towards the tree.

The goblins were busy leaning the ladder against the trunk. Quickly, the fairies darted among the leaves and perched on the branch beside Pushkin. They were hidden from view, but they could hear every word the goblins were saying.

"Get out of my way," the tallest one said, elbowing the others aside. "The bravest should go first."

"In that case, it should be me," said a knock-kneed goblin.

"No, ME!" squawked a goblin with extra-big feet.

He shoved the other two to the

120

pavement and started to climb the ladder.

"Me next!" screeched the knock-kneed goblin.

"Me first!" exclaimed the one wearing the magical helmet, trying to pull the others down. "I'm the bravest of the lot of you!"

As the goblins squabbled, tears welled up in Bailey's eyes.

"I just want you to rescue my kitten," he pleaded.

Kirsty looked up at the kitten, who was gazing at the fairies in surprise.

"I don't think the goblins are going to help Pushkin," she said. "It's up to us."

Chapter Five
A Goblin Pyramid

"Look, Pushkin," said Rachel, pointing to Bailey. "Time to go home."

Pushkin gave a longing little meow.

"All you have to do is make your way down, step by step," said Kirsty. "You can do it, Pushkin. Bailey wants to give you a cuddle."

Pushkin purred and took a cautious little jump to the next branch down.

"That's it!" said Ariana. "Good kitten. Keep going!"

As Pushkin made her way slowly down the tree, Rachel, Kirsty and Ariana kept praising her and telling her how well she was doing. As  the goblins squabbled on the ladder, the kitten grew more and more confident, until at last she reached the bottom of the tree and jumped into Bailey's arms. The three fairies cheered and clapped.

Bailey looked up at the bickering goblins, shook his head and carried Pushkin back into the house. The goblins were too busy arguing about who was bravest to notice that the kitten had gone. Now they were all on the ladder, and it was shaking as they pulled at each other.

"They're going to fall!" cried Ariana.

"Quickly, turn us back into humans," said Kirsty. "This might be our chance to get the helmet."

They all hid behind the tree and Ariana turned them back into humans with a wave of her wand. At the same time, the goblin wearing Ariana's helmet tried to climb over the others to get up the ladder first. Rachel and Kirsty darted out from behind the tree, but they weren't quick enough. The ladder broke and the goblins fell down.

As the goblins tumbled around on the pavement, their helmets came off and rolled into the gutter.

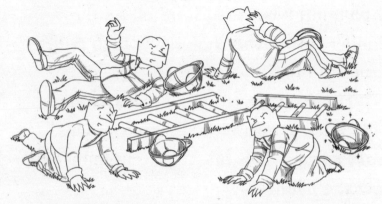

"Quick, grab my helmet!" called Ariana from behind the tree.

But before the girls could reach it, the plump goblin grabbed it and wedged it back on his knobbly head. The girls slipped back behind the tree before they were spotted.

"We have to get that kitten," said the knock-kneed goblin. "If we don't, Jack Frost will say we haven't done the job!"

"Well, how are we supposed to do that without a ladder, genius?" asked the plump goblin.

They still hadn't noticed that the kitten had already been rescued. They tried standing on each other's shoulders, with the goblin in the magical helmet on the bottom row. His hands were raised above his head, holding up the goblin on his shoulders.

"This is our chance," Rachel whispered. "While his arms are up, we can just lift the helmet off his head, and he won't be able to grab us."

She tiptoed out from behind the tree, but just then Pushkin raced out through her cat flap and scampered over to the pyramid of goblins. Her fluffy tail brushed against one of the goblins feet and he squealed.

"That tickles!"

"Stop that!"

The pyramid collapsed in a heap of giggling goblins, and the helmet rolled off again. But this time the goblin with the extra-big feet picked it up and tucked it under his arm.

"I'm in charge now," he shouted. "I'm the boss because I've got the special helmet. You all have to line up and look smart – I'm going to inspect you."

Grumpily, the other goblins nudged each other into a wonky row and stood up as straight as they could. The goblin with the magical helmet strutted up and down in front of them, shaking his head and tutting.

"Your buttons are not shiny enough!" he told the knock-kneed goblin. "None of you is wearing the right sort of boots. Why aren't you carrying fire extinguishers?"

"We're not allowed—"

"Silence!" he bellowed. "No answering back! Stand up straight!"

Rachel joined Kirsty behind the tree again.

"It's no good," she said. "They're just not letting go of it."

Kirsty watched Pushkin darting over towards the hoses in the fire engine, and then thought back to the water fight at the fire station.

"I think I've got an idea!" she said.

Chapter Six
Help from a Hose

Kirsty raced over to the fire engine and grabbed one of the hoses, quickly followed by Rachel.

"Turn it on!' cried Ariana, hovering between them.

Rachel turned the wheel valve and a huge, powerful jet of water shot out of the hose so fast that it made the girls stagger backwards. It took all their strength to aim the water at the pompous, big-footed goblin, who now had the magical helmet on his head.

"Aim for the helmet!" Rachel exclaimed.

The goblins shrieked as the ice-cold water drenched them, and then the girls hit their target. The helmet flew off the goblin's head and Ariana swooped through the air to catch it.

At once, the helmet shrank to fairy size.
Rachel turned the hose off and she and
Kirsty stood there, panting, as the goblins
stared at them with open mouths.

"You can't take that!" wailed the goblin
with the extra-big feet. "What are we
going to tell Jack Frost?"

"He'll be ever so cross," said the
knock-kneed goblin, starting to bite his
fingernails.

"You don't always have to do all the
naughty things he tells you to do," said
Rachel.

"But we *like* being naughty," the tallest
goblin said in a sad voice.

Kirsty couldn't help but feel a bit sorry
for them. She whispered an idea to
Ariana. The little fairy looked surprised,
but she waved her wand and four toy fire

engines appeared in front of the goblins, with real working pedals and padded seats. Instantly, the goblins' frowns were replaced with excited smiles and whoops of joy. They leaped into the fire engines and pedalled away down the street.

"Nee-naw, nee-naw!" they bellowed at top volume.

"They've forgotten all about Jack Frost," said Rachel with a grin.

"I wish I could do the same!" Ariana
sighed, but she was smiling. "Girls, thank
you so much for helping me to find my
magical helmet. I can't wait to show
the other Helping Fairies that we've got
another of our magical objects back."

"We'll find all of them, we promise,"
Kirsty replied.

With a last
wave, Ariana
disappeared back
to Fairyland and
the girls shared a
happy smile. Jack
Frost wasn't going
to find it as easy
as he had thought
to cause trouble
in Tippington!

A little later, the girls were back at the
fire station and the open day was in full
swing. Rachel and Kirsty had called Aunt
Lesley and told her that they had found
the missing fire engine. Isobel had come
to pick it up, and the girls had fun riding
in it and learning what the fire engine
driver had to do.

The official demonstration was very
interesting. The girls and Aunt Lesley
watched and gasped with the rest of
the spectators as Isobel led the other
firefighters up a ladder to rescue a
mannequin. They did it perfectly – with
no water fights!

"Isobel's so brave," said Aunt Lesley. "I
think she and the other firefighters were
just playing a little joke on us earlier."

Rachel and Kirsty smiled and nodded,

but they also squeezed each other's hand, enjoying sharing their secret with each other. After the demonstration, they hurried over to congratulate Isobel.

"You were amazing," said Rachel.

"So brave," added Kirsty. "I hope I would be that brave if I saw a fire."

"Thank you for the compliment," said Isobel, "but the bravest and best thing you could do would be to call the fire brigade. It's part of our job to deal with fires and help people."

"And kittens up trees?" asked Rachel with a grin.

"Sometimes," said Isobel, laughing.

Rachel looked into the main building and saw the sunlight glinting on the shiny silver pole. She took a deep breath.

"Isobel," she said, feeling a little shy, "would it be possible to have a go at sliding down the pole? Just once?"

Isobel threw back her head and laughed.

"Of course," she said. "I should have asked if you wanted to try it – everyone always does!"

She gave the girls fire helmets to wear and led them up the stairs to the top of the pole.

"Now, don't be scared," she said. "I'll go first so you can see how it's done."

The girls watched Isobel carefully, and then Rachel zoomed down the pole with an excited squeal. Kirsty followed quickly, laughing as Isobel caught her at the bottom.

"That is so much fun!" she exclaimed.

"Try it, Aunt Lesley!" Rachel called up.

Her aunt shrieked with delight as she slid down the fire pole too.

"I think I might get one installed at the surgery," she joked. "It might help to cheer up my poorly patients!"

Still laughing, they all said goodbye
to Isobel and promised to see her at the
Tippington Helper of the Year Award
ceremony.

As Aunt Lesley went to fetch the car,
Rachel and Kirsty
shared a happy
smile.

"We've
already got
two of the
Helping
Fairies'
magical objects
back from Jack
Frost," said Rachel.
"Martha and Ariana
must be glad that they can help
people again."

"Yes, but Perrie and Lulu still need us," said Kirsty. "We have to find the siren and whistle before the ceremony."

"It feels even more important after today," said Rachel, looking around at all the smiling faces around her. "We have to make sure that community heroes like Isobel can carry on helping others."

"We will," said Kirsty. "We might not be able to fight fires, but I'd say we can definitely help the Helping Fairies – and I can't wait for the next adventure!"

Story Three
Perrie the
Paramedic Fairy

Chapter One
Marathon Man

"I've never seen the park so busy," said Rachel Walker, gazing around.

It was a sunny spring morning, and Tippington Park was packed with people. Everyone was there to watch the start of the Tippington Town Half Marathon.

"I hope your dad wins," said Rachel's best friend, Kirsty Tate.

Kirsty was staying with Rachel for the spring half-term holidays. They both looked across to where Mr Walker was warming up for the race. He was wearing a white vest top and running

trousers. The number seven was pinned to his vest.

"He's in with a good chance," said Rachel. "He's been training every day for months! But he always says it's not about winning."

"It's about taking part," agreed Mrs Walker, who was standing behind them. "Your dad has already raised lots of money for charity."

The girls gazed around at the crowds of runners and spectators. Everyone looked happy and excited. The half-marathon was an important event for Tippington Town. People looked forward to it all year long.

"I wonder if we'll see any of our fairy friends today," said Rachel.

"Or any goblins," Kirsty added. "We should keep our eyes peeled – the Tippington Helper of the Year Award is being presented tomorrow and we still need to find two of the Helping Fairies' magical objects."

The nominations for the Tippington Helper of the Year Award had been announced at the start of the week. It was a very important local prize that recognised the special people in the community whose job was to help others. This year it was especially exciting for Rachel and Kirsty, because Rachel's Aunt Lesley was one of the nominees.

She was an excellent doctor, and the girls felt sure that she would win. But they were the only humans who knew that the award ceremony might go very wrong indeed.

Two days ago, Jack Frost had stolen the magical objects that belonged to the Helping Fairies. He had sent his goblins to the human world with the fairies' magical objects and ordered them to do the jobs of the award nominees. He wanted to take the credit for himself so he could win the award without actually helping anyone.

Kirsty and Rachel had already helped Martha the Doctor Fairy and Ariana the Firefighter Fairy to get their magical objects back, but there were still two left to find, and the ceremony was getting closer. The girls felt sure that Jack Frost and his goblins would be planning to cause as much trouble as possible for the award nominees.

"Do you think the goblins might be here?" asked Rachel.

"We know that they're hanging around Tippington to take over from the award nominees," said Kirsty. "There are bound to be some of the nominees here today. I bet the goblins won't be far away."

They looked around, but for now, everything seemed calm and goblin-free. Then they saw Aunt Lesley coming out of the first-aid station. It looked peaceful and the ambulance beside the station was standing quiet. Aunt Lesley spotted the girls and came over to join them beside the track, smiling.

"Good morning, girls!" she said. "I've come to cheer for your dad, Rachel."

Mr Walker was just coming over to join them, and he heard what she said.

"Thanks, Lesley," he said with a grin. "It's helpful to know I've got so much support – it makes me determined to run my fastest!"

Just then a loudspeaker crackled.

"Would all runners please make their way to the starting line?" said a loud, echoing voice. "The race is about to start."

Mr Walker hugged the girls and then headed over to join the other competitors.

"Good luck!" called Rachel, Kirsty, Mrs Walker and Aunt Lesley.

There were so many people crowding

around that it was hard to see the person who was starting the race. But they heard the crack of a starting pistol. A huge cheer went up as the runners surged forward.

"They're off!" shouted Rachel, jumping up and down in excitement. "Go on, Dad, you can do it!"

Chapter Two
Paramedics in a Panic

The girls and Aunt Lesley cheered loudly as Mr Walker ran past them.

"I guess you girls are waiting here to see the end of the race?" asked Aunt Lesley.

Rachel and Kirsty nodded.

"Are you going to wait with us?"

Rachel asked. "We could get ice creams
– Mum said that there are usually lots of
food stalls around."

"I'd love to, but my patients need me,"
said Aunt Lesley. "I have to hurry back
to my surgery."

"No wonder your patients love you,"
said Kirsty. "You're very dedicated to
them."

"You're bound to win Tippington
Helper of the Year!" Rachel added.

"There are lots of people who help
others in Tippington," smiled Aunt
Lesley, glancing over at the first-aid
station. "My friends the paramedics,
for example."

"What do they do?" Kirsty asked.

"They work on board ambulances
and give people first aid to make them

feel better," Aunt Lesley replied. "They're here today to look after any runners who might get injured during the race. They have to think and act fast, because people are depending on them. In fact, the senior paramedic has been nominated for the Tippington Helper of the Year Award, just like me."

The girls glanced at each other. If the goblins were nearby, they would certainly be somewhere close to an award nominee. They had to find a way to get closer to the first-aid station.

"Aunt Lesley, might you have time to introduce us to the paramedics before you go to work?" Rachel asked. "We'd love to find out more about what they do."

Aunt Lesley looked at her watch and smiled.

"I've got five minutes," she said. "I'm so pleased that you both want to know more about helping jobs. I enjoy my work very much, and I know that the paramedics do too."

She led the girls to the first-aid station and walked up to the man and woman wearing dark-green uniforms. They were checking their supplies when the girls arrived.

"Colin and Tiana, this is my niece Rachel and her friend Kirsty," said Aunt Lesley. "Girls, Colin is the senior paramedic I was telling you about."

"Welcome!" said Colin with a friendly smile. "Would you like to see the inside of our ambulance?"

"Ooh, yes please!" said Rachel and Kirsty together.

"I must go," said Aunt Lesley. "I'll leave you in Colin and Tiana's capable hands."

They said goodbye to Aunt Lesley and then Tiana and Colin led them into the ambulance.

"There are so many machines!" said Kirsty, gazing around in wonder. There were dials, switches and screens everywhere she looked.

"We've got equipment for almost

every sort of injury," said Tiana. "This is a heart monitor, and this is oxygen for people who are having trouble breathing."

"What's in all your little cupboards?" asked Rachel, looking at the cubbyholes above and around the trolley bed.

"All our medical kits are stored in there, with things like bandages, plasters, slings and gauze," said Colin. "It's also where we keep back-up supplies, in case we run out of anything."

He showed them a blood-pressure cuff and an inflatable splint.

He had just picked up a spinal collar
when they heard someone calling for
help outside the ambulance. They all
hurried out and saw one of the runners
standing outside the first-aid station,
holding her knee.

"Are you OK?" asked Kirsty, hurrying
over to her.

"What happened?" asked Rachel.

"I tripped over a
stone and grazed
my knee," said
the woman,
wincing in
pain. "If
I can get
it treated
quickly, I can
still join the race."

Rachel and Kirsty looked around, but to their surprise Colin and Tiana were still standing beside the ambulance. They weren't even looking at the injured woman.

"Colin?" called Kirsty. "This lady needs some help."

She expected him to dash over to her at once, but Colin glanced at the woman's knee and then looked away again.

He had turned rather green in the face, and he looked as if he might be sick.

"I can't bear to look," he said. "Suddenly the sight of blood makes me feel ill."

"Tiana, can you help?" Rachel asked.

"Oh my goodness, it's an emergency!" cried Tiana, opening her eyes very wide. "We have to do something! I can't remember how to treat a graze! Where's the kit? How do I start?"

She was panting and getting very red in the face. Then she burst into tears, sat down and put her head in her hands.

"She's panicking," said the runner, sounding confused. "That's not very helpful."

Rachel and Kirsty exchanged a quick, worried glance. Paramedics should be quick-thinking and calm in an emergency, and they certainly shouldn't turn green at the sight of blood!

"I'm sure Colin and Tiana are acting strangely because Jack Frost has taken the Helping Fairies' magical objects," said Kirsty in a low voice. "It's so unfair. He wants to be Helper of the Year without actually helping anybody, and he's spoiling things for everyone else."

"We have to try to get Colin and Tiana back to normal," said Rachel. "But first, let's help this poor lady. I know what to do about a grazed knee – I've had so many of them!"

"Me too," said Kirsty with a smile. "I'll go and get the medical kit from the ambulance – I remember where Colin and Tiana keep it."

While Tiana groaned and Colin leaned against the side of the ambulance, Kirsty fetched a small medical kit. Rachel used a sterile wipe to clean the graze. Then Kirsty gently put some antiseptic cream onto the woman's knee.

"Now we just need a plaster," she said. "Look – it's the last one in the kit."

As soon as the plaster was on her knee, the woman thanked them and sprinted

off to join the race.

"Let's put some more plasters in the kit," said Rachel. "I saw a box in the ambulance earlier."

Colin and Tiana were still recovering from their shock, so the girls jumped into the ambulance and went over to the cupboard where they had seen the plasters. Kirsty took out the box. As she opened it, Perrie the Paramedic Fairy fluttered out!

Chapter Three
A Help or a Hindrance?

"Hello, Perrie!" exclaimed Rachel. "Have you come to see the marathon?"

"No," said Perrie with panic in her voice. "Oh girls, please will you come and help me? Jack Frost is causing havoc!"

Before the girls could reply, they

heard voices outside the ambulance. Kirsty peeped out and saw that two more people had arrived at the first aid station – a little boy with a nosebleed and a runner holding his side. Colin had screwed up his eyes so he didn't have to look at the blood, and Tiana had buried her head in her hands as if it was all too much for her.

"He looks as if he's got a stitch," said Rachel, coming to stand beside Kirsty. "Oh dear, they both need our help. The paramedics don't know what to do."

"That's because Jack Frost still has my magical flashing siren," said Perrie. "The best way to help them is to come with me. Don't forget, time in the human world stands still while you're in Fairyland."

"Then let's go!" said Rachel at once.
"We can't let Jack Frost make any more
trouble!"

"Oh, thank you!" Perrie exclaimed.

She waved her wand, and a long green
ribbon
twisted out
of the tip.
It coiled
around the
girls, tying
itself into
bows and
rippling
like a wave.
Rachel and
Kirsty shrank to fairy size,
and beautiful wings carried them
twirling into the air.

Then, in a sparkling burst of rainbow colours, they were whisked away to Fairyland.

With sparkles of fairy dust fading around them, Rachel and Kirsty found themselves standing among a group of toadstool houses. They could see the Fairyland Palace on the hill in the distance. As they looked around, the doors of the little houses opened and

a few curious fairies peeped out. The girls recognised some of them at once.

"Look, there's Francesca the Football Fairy!" exclaimed Kirsty. "Hi, Francesca! Oh, what's wrong with her poor foot?"

Francesca's right foot was in a plaster cast. They saw Bethany the Ballet Fairy with a bandaged toe and Alesha the Acrobat Fairy with a bandage on the top of her head. Then Bertram, the frog footman, hobbled past on crutches.

In fact, every single fairy they saw
seemed to have some sort of injury.

"What's happened to everyone?" asked
Rachel in a shocked voice. "Bertram, are
you all right?"

Bertram smiled
at her.

"We're all fine,"
he said. "No one
is really hurt at
all. But Jack Frost
has been zooming
around in an
ambulance with
the light flashing and
the siren blaring. He's ordered his goblins
to bandage everyone up, even though
they're not injured."

"But why?" asked Kirsty.

"He's pretending to be helpful," said Perrie with a sigh. "He takes the credit for helping everyone, even though he isn't helping at all. He's just being a big hindrance! Francesca can't play football with a cast on her foot. Bethany can't dance and Alesha can't stand on her head."

"It's impossible for me to open doors while I've got these crutches," Bertram added. "I keep tripping people up."

"Jack Frost loves thinking of new ways to cause trouble," said Rachel. "We won't let him spoil things for everyone!"

"Wait," said Kirsty, putting her head on one side. "Can you hear something?"

They all listened. *NEE-NAW! NEE-NAW!* It was a siren, and it was growing louder and louder.

"It's Jack Frost," said Bertram with a groan. "He's coming back with his awful ambulance. Hide!"

As Bertram dived behind a rose bush,

an ice-blue ambulance came zooming
over the hill towards them. Its light
was flashing to show that there was an
emergency, and the girls could see that
Jack Frost was hunched over the steering
wheel. Five goblins were piled up in the
passenger seat, clinging on to each other
and looking terrified. Each goblin had
a big red cross painted on his knobbly
green forehead.

"He's going much too fast," said Kirsty
as the ambulance hurtled past. "I hope
he doesn't have an accident. It's lucky
his siren and light warned us that he was
coming."

"That's not his light," cried Perrie in a desperate voice. "It's my magical flashing siren!"

Chapter Four
Siren in the Snow

"We have to help Perrie get her siren back," said Rachel, turning towards Kirsty.

But Kirsty was already fluttering into the air.

"Come on!" she exclaimed to her friends. "Let's chase them!"

Rachel and Perrie zoomed towards
her, and the three fairies flew after the
ambulance as fast as they could. They
zipped over toadstool houses, up hills
and down into daisy-strewn valleys.
They were going so quickly that
everything below looked blurry. The
girls grinned at each other as they urged
their wings to flap faster and faster.
They zoomed towards the very edges of
Fairyland, leaving the exquisite palace
behind in the distance. Perrie took the
lead, her blonde hair streaming out
behind her as they flew.

"We've almost caught it up!" she cried. "Keep going!"

When the ambulance reached an extremely steep hill, it slowed down slightly. Ice was sparkling on the road, and they could see Jack Frost's castle in the distance. The hills ahead were glittering with snow and ice. Panting, the fairies caught up with the ambulance and flew right above it, trying to decide what to do.

"Let's just swoop down and take the siren from the top of the ambulance," Rachel suggested.

Perrie shook her head. "It's going too fast," she said. "We need the ambulance to stop."

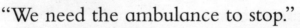

"I've got an idea!" said Kirsty. "Jack Frost might stop if he thinks there's a patient to treat. We just have to get ahead of the ambulance."

They all put on a burst of speed and passed the ambulance, flying over the hill so they were hidden from sight on the other side. Kirsty swooped down and landed on the steep, snowy hill.

"Stay high up so they can't see you!" she called to Rachel and Perrie. "I'll try to get the ambulance to stop."

Kirsty kneeled on the snowy ground and held one of her wings as if it were injured. She hung her head to pretend that she was crying.

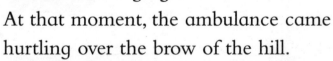

At that moment, the ambulance came hurtling over the brow of the hill.

"Help! Please stop!" Kirsty cried out, waving her arm.

The ambulance screeched to a halt and the window was wound down. Jack Frost's spiky head poked out and he glared at her.

"What's the matter with you?" he snapped.

"My wing needs to be bandaged," Kirsty replied. "Can you help me?"

Jack Frost leaned across, opened the passenger door and then shoved the goblins out into the snow.

"Bandage her wing," he barked at them. "Do it now, so I get even more credit for being helpful! And hurry up – I want my lunch."

Complaining in loud voices, the goblins opened the back of the ambulance and clambered in to find their bandaging kit.

Meanwhile, Rachel fluttered carefully
down towards the magical flashing siren.
She reached out her hand towards it, but
just at that moment, Jack Frost turned it
on again. *NEE-NAW! NEE-NAW!*

Startled, Rachel
sprang back
and tumbled
off the
front
of the
ambulance.
As she
fluttered her
wings to stop
herself from falling,
she accidentally knocked against the
windscreen. Turning in midair, she saw
Jack Frost's cold blue eyes glaring at her.

"Quickly, grab the siren!" Rachel yelled.

She flew up and Perrie dived towards it, but Jack Frost reached up one of his long arms and snatched it off the roof of the ambulance.

"I know exactly what you want!" he bawled at the top of his voice. "You're not getting this siren from me – I'm having way too much fun with it!"

Chapter Five
Bruised Bottoms

"That siren belongs to Perrie," said Kirsty, jumping up. "Give it back to her right now!"

Jack Frost blew a big raspberry at her and then leaped out of the ambulance and started to run.

"Be careful!" Kirsty called after him.

"This hill is really steep and slippery — you might fall and get hurt!"

"That sort of thing only happens to weedy fairies," sneered Jack Frost with an unpleasant laugh. "I'm so clever, I can run as fast as I want and still not fall over."

He sprinted off down the hill, and the three fairies zoomed after him. Behind them, the goblins started yelling and wailing.

"Don't leave us behind!"

"Come back!"

"Slow down!" cried Rachel. "Be careful!"

But Jack only laughed at all the shouting and ran faster. He looked up to check where the fairies were, and then disaster struck! He slipped on a large patch of ice and slid forwards down the steep hill, scrabbling and yelling. His arms whirled around like windmills and he squealed and screeched, but nothing could stop him.

"What can we do?" Kirsty called out.

Before they could think of a plan, Jack Frost struck a bump, flew into the air and landed on his bottom on a frozen puddle. *CRACK!* The ice broke and Jack Frost's bottom sank into the freezing water.

"YOWWWWCH!" he squealed,
struggling to his feet. "My poor bony
bottom! This is agony! I'm hurt! Call the
doctor! Call the air ambulance!"

He clutched his
bottom with one
hand and held on
to the siren with
the other. The
fairies hovered
in front of him.

"You can't be
too badly hurt
if you're able to
move around,"
said Perrie. "I
expect it's just a bruise."

"Just a bruise?" Jack Frost repeated in
outrage. "I'm probably scarred for life!"

Just then they heard a high-pitched screeching sound. The goblins were sliding down the hill and squealing at the tops of their voices. They hit the same bump, flew through the air and landed on Jack Frost. They all fell into a heap, arms and legs flailing around.

"My bottom!" cried one of the goblins. "Never mind *your* bottom, what about *my* bottom?" bellowed Jack Frost.

"Listen to me," said Rachel. "Please listen!"

But the goblins and Jack Frost were making so much noise that they didn't hear her. She took a deep breath and spoke in her loudest voice. "Perrie can make you all better!"

Everyone fell silent and stared at her.

"All you have to do is give her back the magical siren," Rachel went on.

At once, the goblins set up a loud clamour.

"Give it back! My bottom is throbbing!"

"Give it back! My arm hurts!"

"Give it back! Give it back!"

Chapter Six
The Finishing Line

Faced by five glaring goblins, Jack Frost hesitated.

"Perrie is the only one who can help you," said Kirsty.

With a sigh and a frown, Jack Frost held out the siren and Perrie took it. A big smile spread across her face as she hugged the siren to her chest.

"Now you have to keep your end of the bargain," said Jack Frost.

"I *always* keep my promises," said Perrie.

She waved her wand over Jack Frost and the goblins. At once Jack Frost jumped to his feet, quickly followed by the goblins. But they didn't say thank you to Perrie. Jack Frost just glared at the fairies.

"You pesky fairies have spoiled everything again," he grumbled. "How am I supposed to win the Helper of the Year Award without the magical flashing siren?"

"Well, you helped by giving it back to Perrie," said Rachel. "That's much more helpful than bandaging people up when there's nothing wrong with them."

Jack looked a bit less cross for a moment. Then he turned, whipping his cloak around him, and stamped off through the snow. The goblins stumbled after him, leaving a trail of large footprints behind them.

"I'm so happy we got the siren back," said Perrie. "I've been very worried about all the paramedics. Now everything will get back to normal."

She looked back at the ice-blue ambulance at the top of the hill. Jack Frost had forgotten about it now that he didn't have the siren.

"The ambulance can't stay there," she said.

She waved her wand and the ambulance disappeared. Then Perrie turned to Rachel and Kirsty and threw her arms around them.

"You're both amazing friends," she said with a beaming smile. "I couldn't have stopped Jack Frost without you. How can I ever thank you enough?"

"We're just happy that we were helpful," said Kirsty. "It feels good to know that everything's back to normal."

"I wonder if Colin and Tiana will be feeling better when we get back to Tippington," Rachel said.

"You'll find out in a minute," Perrie replied. "It's time for me to send you home."

Rachel and Kirsty hugged the delighted fairy, and she waved her wand. The snow swirled around them and they closed their eyes. A few seconds later, they heard the distant chatter of a large crowd and found that they were back in the ambulance in Tippington Park.

"Rachel?" called Colin's voice. "Kirsty?"

The girls hurried out of the ambulance and saw Colin smiling at them. He was just closing his medical kit. Kirsty spotted the boy with the nosebleed walking away.

"Was he all right?" she asked.

"Oh yes," said Colin. "Just a little nosebleed – nothing to get upset about."

"So you don't mind the sight of blood?" Rachel asked.

Colin laughed. "I wouldn't be a very good paramedic if I were squeamish!"

Rachel and Kirsty shared a secret smile as Tiana came out of the first-aid station with the runner who had had a stitch. He thanked her and sprinted off, smiling.

"He's all better," said Tiana in a happy, calm voice. "Although the runners are starting to finish the race, so he'll have to be quick!"

Rachel glanced over to the track and

saw Mr Walker running towards the finishing line.

"Dad's nearly finished!" she cried. "Come on, let's go and meet him!"

They said goodbye to Colin and Tiana, and then darted over to the finishing line. Mrs Walker was standing there, and she waved when she saw the girls.

"I've got a towel and a bottle of water ready for your dad," she said. "Do you want to give them to him?"

A few seconds later, Mr Walker

crossed the finishing line and saw
Rachel and Kirsty jumping up and down
in excitement.

"Hurray!" they both shouted. "You did
it! Hurray!"

Red in the face, laughing and puffing,
Mr Walker took the towel and the bottle
of water. He had a long drink and put
the towel around his neck.

"That's just what I needed," he said.
"You're both wonderful helpers. Thank
you!"

As Mrs Walker gave him a hug, Rachel
and Kirsty smiled at each other.

"It's fun to help people," said Rachel.

"Especially the fairies," Kirsty agreed
quietly. "And now there's only one more
magical object to find."

"We just have to make sure we find
it before tomorrow's Helper of the Year
Award ceremony," said
Rachel. "Do you
think we can?"

Kirsty put her
arm around her best
friend's shoulders
and gave her a
squeeze.

"I *know* we can," she said. "The fairies are depending on us to help them, and we won't let them down!"

The End

Now it's time for Kirsty and Rachel to help ...

Lulu the Lifeguard Fairy

Read on for a sneak peek ...

"Finally, I would like to thank my wonderful patients, who have been kind enough to nominate me for this award," said Aunt Lesley. "I look forward to continuing to help them."

On the sofa in the Walkers' sitting room, Kirsty Tate and Rachel Walker clapped with enthusiasm. Kirsty was visiting her best friend for the spring half term, and Rachel's Aunt Lesley was staying there too. She was a respected local doctor, and the girls had really enjoyed spending time with her during the holiday.

"Do you think that sounds all right, girls?" asked Aunt Lesley, looking nervous. "I feel a bit silly practising what I'll say if I win the award."

Aunt Lesley had been nominated for the Tippington Helper of the Year Award. It was a local prize that rewarded the special people in the community who had a job helping others, and the ceremony was that evening at Tippington Town Hall.

"You definitely need to have a speech ready," said Rachel. "You're bound to win!"

"I'm not so sure," said Aunt Lesley with a laugh. "You've met most of the other nominees. They're all brilliant at their jobs."

Kirsty and Rachel nodded.

"Isobel the firefighter and Colin the paramedic are wonderful," said Rachel.

"And I'm sure Mark the lifeguard is amazing," Kirsty added. "But we want *you* to win!"

Aunt Lesley smiled at them.

"I'm so pleased that I've had your company this week," she said. "You two always seem to be having fun."

Just then, they heard the doorbell ring.

"That must be Bailey," said Rachel, jumping up. "Sorry, Aunt Lesley, but we have to go now. Bailey's mum is taking us all to the local pool."

Bailey was the boy who lived next door. The girls had helped to rescue his kitten, Pushkin, a few days earlier, and his mum was taking them to a swimming lesson as a way of saying thank you. Rachel and Kirsty said goodbye to Aunt

Lesley and scooped up their swimming bags as they headed for the door. When they opened it, Bailey was standing there with a big smile on his face.

"Ready for our lesson?" he asked.

"We can't wait," said Kirsty. "Let's go!"

They had a fun ride in Bailey's mum's car, singing along to the radio at the tops of their voices. They arrived at the leisure centre and dashed to the changing rooms to get into their swimsuits. Then they went to join the other children at the shallow end of the pool.

"Isn't it brilliant that Mark's been nominated for the Tippington Helper of the Year Award?" said a blonde-haired girl in a red swimsuit. "He's such a great swimming teacher – I really think he deserves to win."

"I thought he worked as a lifeguard," said Rachel.

"He takes our lessons too," said the girl with a smile. "He thinks it's really important to learn how to swim."

"He told me that he's seen lots of people who can't swim well get into trouble in the water," said a boy in blue trunks. "Working as a lifeguard was what made him want to learn to teach swimming."

"He sounds great," said Kirsty with a big smile. "I can't wait for the lesson to start!"

Just then, a man wearing red swimming shorts came striding down the poolside towards them. He had a yellow whistle around his neck and grinned at the waiting children.

"OK, everyone, I hope you're feeling

energetic!" he said in a booming voice. "Today I'm going to show you how to do the front crawl. For this stroke you have to think about kicking, paddling and breathing all at the same time. Watch me first and then jump into the pool and we'll all try it together."

He jumped into the shallow end of the pool, but instead of starting to swim, he just thrashed about. Spluttering and shaking, he lurched towards the ladder and hauled himself out of the pool.

"Was that a new stroke?" asked Bailey. "I've never seen it before."

Rachel and Kirsty exchanged a worried glance, and Mark looked embarrassed.

"That wasn't a swimming stroke at all," he said, panting. "I've forgotten how to swim! I'm sorry but I can't take a swimming lesson if I don't trust myself in the water. I'm going to have to cancel the lesson and close the pool. There are no other lifeguards available to take over from me."

Looking very disappointed, the other children in the class wandered over to the bench to collect their towels. Rachel and Kirsty paused and watched Mark sit down on the poolside and put his head in his hands.

"Poor Mark," said Rachel. "What on earth could have made him forget how to swim?"

The others were already walking into the changing rooms. As the girls went to pick up their towels, Kirsty drew in her breath sharply.

"Look at your towel," she exclaimed. "It's glowing!"

"It's magic," said Rachel, and the best friends shared a happy smile.

Even though they had been on many magical adventures, they always felt a thrill of excitement when they had a visit from a fairy. Rachel picked up her towel and saw Lulu the Lifeguard Fairy sitting cross-legged on the bench.

"Hello, Lulu!" said Rachel. "What are you doing here?"

The little fairy jumped up, fluttering her wings. She was wearing a yellow T-shirt tied up at the front into a knot, a pair of red shorts and pink trainers that matched her whistle.

"I've come to ask for your help," she said, shaking back her shiny brown hair. "I have to find a way to get my magical rescue float back from Jack Frost and his goblins."

On the first day of Kirsty's visit to Tippington, Martha the Doctor Fairy had whisked the girls to Fairyland to meet the other Helping Fairies. Jack Frost had stolen their magical objects, and without them the fairies couldn't help everyday heroes like Aunt Lesley do their jobs.

"We'll do whatever you need us to do," said Rachel.

Read **Lulu the Lifeguard Fairy** to find out what adventures are in store for Kirsty and Rachel!

Discover all four of the Helping Fairies stories

Martha
the Doctor Fairy
Daisy Meadows

Ariana
the Firefighter Fairy
Daisy Meadows

Perrie
the Paramedic Fairy
Daisy Meadows

Lulu
the Lifeguard Fairy
Daisy Meadows

Find them all at rainbowmagicbooks.co.uk

Calling all parents, carers and teachers!
The Rainbow Magic fairies are here to help
your child enter the magical world of reading.
Whatever reading stage they are at, there's
a Rainbow Magic book for everyone!
Here is Lydia the Reading Fairy's guide to
supporting your child's journey at all levels.

Starting Out

Our Rainbow Magic Beginner Readers are perfect for first-time readers who are just beginning to develop reading skills and confidence. Approved by teachers, they contain a full range of educational levelling, as well as lively full-colour illustrations.

Developing Readers

Rainbow Magic Early Readers contain longer stories and wider vocabulary for building stamina and growing confidence. These are adaptations of our most popular Rainbow Magic stories, specially developed for younger readers in conjunction with an Early Years reading consultant, with full-colour illustrations.

Going Solo

The Rainbow Magic chapter books – a mixture of series and one-off specials – contain accessible writing to encourage your child to venture into reading independently. These highly collectible and much-loved magical stories inspire a love of reading to last a lifetime.

www.rainbowmagicbooks.co.uk

"Rainbow Magic got my daughter reading chapter books. Great sparkly covers, cute fairies and traditional stories full of magic that she found impossible to put down" - Mother of Edie (6 years)

"Florence LOVES the Rainbow Magic books. She really enjoys reading now" - Mother of Florence (6 years)

Read along the Reading Rainbow!

Well done – you have completed the book!

This book was worth 2 stars.

See how far you have climbed on the Reading Rainbow opposite.
The more books you read, the more stars you can colour in
and the closer you will be to becoming a Royal Fairy!

Do you want to print your own Reading Rainbow?

1) Go to the Rainbow Magic website

2) Download and print out the poster

3) Colour in a star for every book you finish
and climb the Reading Rainbow

4) For every step up the rainbow,
you can download your very own certificate

There's all this and lots more at
rainbowmagicbooks.co.uk

You'll find activities, stories, a special newsletter
AND you can search for the fairy with your name!